Dedicated to my wife, Sarah, my son, Theo, and our dog, Frida,
for keeping me company while I made this book.
Now let's explore together!

In memory of Laban Carrick Hill.

Published by Roaring Brook Press
Roaring Brook Press is a division of Holtzbrinck Publishing Holdings Limited Partnership
120 Broadway, New York, NY 10271 · mackids.com

Our books may be purchased in bulk for promotional, educational, or business use.
Please contact your local bookseller or the Macmillan Corporate and Premium Sales Department at
(800) 221-7945 ext. 5442 or by email at MacmillanSpecialMarkets@macmillan.com.

Library of Congress Cataloging-in-Publication Data is available.

First edition, 2022
The illustrations for this book were created in Procreate.
This book was edited by Mekisha Telfer and Connie Hsu and designed by Aram Kim.
The production editor was Mia Moran, and the production manager was Allene Cassagnol.

Printed in China by RR Donnelley Asia Printing Solutions Ltd., Dongguan City, Guangdong Province

ISBN 978-1-62672-294-1 (hardcover)

1 3 5 7 9 10 8 6 4 2

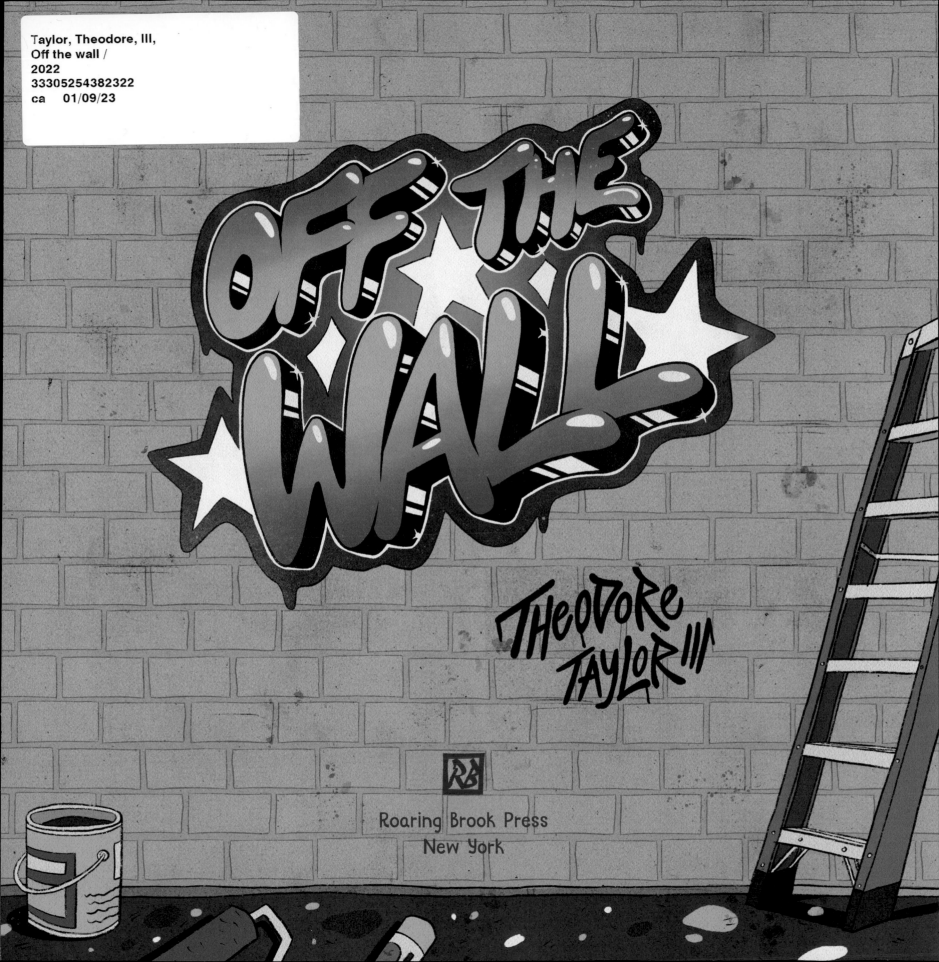

OFF THE WALL

THEODORE TAYLOR III

Roaring Brook Press
New York

Mom and Dad were so excited, moving from one end of the country to the other to trade our fast, busy city life for a small, quiet one far away.

We pulled up to our big, new house
full of big, echoing, empty rooms.

I missed the comfort of our small, cozy apartment and the sounds of the busy streets outside.

At school, I felt like an outsider—
like I was from another planet.

I was ready to take the first spacecraft home.
Until I spotted something on the side of an old building...

Shapes moving in every direction, letters weaving in and out, bright colors jumping off the wall. It was like a language from another planet that only I could understand.

Graffiti.

It reminded me of home—loud and energetic. There, the streets were full of people moving in every direction, day or night. The city itself was a work of art, always ready to show me something new.

That night my dreams were full of graffiti, as if someone in town was trying to send me a message—and it was my job to find out who.

The next morning, I had a surprise visitor: my cousin, Lincoln, who lived down the street.

Lincoln offered to show me around. Excited to see the writing on the wall again, I asked him to take me back downtown.

Only to find that it was gone.

The graffiti had been painted overnight
in shades of dull white and gray.

But Lincoln wasn't worried . . .

He knew graffiti was hiding everywhere. Tags in the alley, stickers on street signs, stencils on the corner, throw-ups on moving vans, murals in parking lots reaching high into the sky.

The farther away from town we walked, the more graffiti we found. On a hill overlooking railroad tracks, a freight train passed by, every car wrapped in graffiti. It was like an art gallery in motion.

Lincoln was ready to head home, but it felt like we were inching close to something. On the horizon was what looked like an abandoned factory.

But I could hear the rattle and hiss of spray cans and the faint thump of music playing. I peeked into the front door.

Inside we discovered dozens of artists painting every inch of the building's walls. We had stepped into another world.

They each had their own unique style and technique.
They used tools like paint rollers, stencils, brushes, and,
of course, spray cans.

Some were lifted high toward the ceiling
on cherry pickers.

At the far end of the building, I noticed a girl about my age, painting by her mother's side.

I nervously introduced myself and asked what was going on.

She explained that the town had given the building to local artists to paint whatever they wanted.

Soon they would repair it and turn the building into a space for the community.

She handed me a can and asked
if I wanted to help.

AUTHOR'S NOTE

Sarah Schultz-Taylor

DISCLAIMER: I am not a graffiti artist. But I do have a strong appreciation for the craft that is inspiring, mysterious, and, yes, often illegal.

Growing up in the small city of Roanoke, Virginia, didn't provide me with much exposure to graffiti. I will admit that one of my earliest obsessions with it started in the form of *Jet Grind Radio*, a video game for the Sega Dreamcast about tagging your turf while competing with rival graffiti crews, and pulling off tricks on rollerblades in a colorful, fictional version of Tokyo, Japan.

I had never seen or heard anything like it, and it stuck with me immediately. Not the most authentic entry point, but that is where my interest in "underground" hip-hop and graffiti culture took hold.

On high school class trips to New York City, I would take my camera and shoot artsy photos of the dense, urban landscape and graffiti-covered walls that were nowhere to be found in my hometown. I was fascinated. I had the same experience in Washington, D.C., my father's hometown and where my extended family still live. I had visited many times, but when my grandfather took me to the neighborhood of Adams Morgan for the first time, I was amazed by the huge murals and colorful buildings.

Perhaps *Jet Grind Radio* wasn't that far from real life after all.

Back home, my work took on a more urban, street art-influenced style. My interest in urban environments and culture grew. I absorbed documentaries like *Dark Days*, *Wild Style*, and *Style Wars*, in contrast with the quiet county suburb in which I lived. But one of my good friends (Hey, Cody!) spent a lot of time exploring

Washington, D.C.

downtown, finding hidden areas and secret corners of the city. On two occasions he took me and a friend along with him. Camera in hand, I was able to capture another side of the city that I didn't know existed. Old, abandoned, crumbling structures were everywhere. So was graffiti, left like cave paintings of prehistoric origin.

Then and now, when I look at graffiti I wonder: Who painted it? When was it painted? How? Why?

Those same questions arose on a family trip to Italy and our visit to Pompeii, the ancient Roman city buried by the Mount Vesuvius eruption almost 2,000 years ago. There, we saw beautiful uncovered frescoes, architecture, pottery, and other artifacts. But what I enjoyed the most was the ancient graffiti left on walls by everyday people. It offered a glimpse into what they thought and experienced back then, illustrating that they were much like us today. They expressed humor and a universal desire to be noticed.

Graffiti is a sign of life.

I've heard artists contrast graffiti with billboards. They ask: What would you rather see? Advertisements attempting to push you to consume, or a form of artistic expression that inspires you? In 2007, the mayor of São Paulo, Brazil, introduced the Clean City Law, banning billboards from the city. In its place came street art. Murals by the likes of Os Gemeos and Nunca adorned the city. A unique style grew, fostering a collection of artists that influenced

Italy

Toronto, Canada

Montréal, Canada

me early in college and continue to influence me today. Cities providing local artists public spaces to create and be seen can produce great things. It brings a certain sense of identity and culture to a city, in a way billboards might not.

I've seen a wave of cities making space for artists in my travels. Toronto and Montréal were plastered with great art, as was Paris. The cities of Houston, Texas, and Asheville, North Carolina, had dedicated graffiti spaces. When living in D.C., I attended my first street art festival. In Richmond, Virginia, where I currently live, street art festivals are held annually, and as a result, there are fantastic murals all over the city. Many have become iconic, such as the owl mural by Jeff Soto. (It provided a perfect backdrop when my wife and I took our wedding photos.) Those annual street art festivals included one in 2013 at an abandoned bus depot, reopened to pedestrians and covered in art. Unfortunately, it was never meant to be permanent and was later entirely painted over.

That erasure reminded me of my first and last visit to New York City's 5 Pointz, a mecca for graffiti artists and street art enthusiasts. In 2013, the building's new owners made the decision to paint over and demolish it to make way for condominiums. Twenty-one artists later received $6.7 million in damages. That demolition still hurts and confounds me.

Despite community urges to buff away graffiti, this form of art continues to act as a voice for those who feel they don't have one. In the notorious year of 2020, in the wake of the death of George Floyd, protesters took to the streets across the country to make their voices heard. In Richmond, once capital of the Confederacy, there was a concerted effort to remove symbols of oppression. Up and down Monument Avenue, every statue honoring Confederate heroes was defaced with graffiti. I could hear confrontations with the police from my home, several miles away.

When the dust settled, the graffiti-covered pedestal of Confederate General Robert E. Lee provided a space for communal healing and had been transformed into a new symbol of unity and justice, even making its way to the cover of *National Geographic* magazine. In the end, every statue—save that of Black American tennis great Arthur Ashe, who was born and raised in Richmond—was removed. Only the graffiti-covered pedestals remain.

My goal with this book isn't to push children to tag up their neighborhoods, but to inspire those who feel like outsiders to find their voice and place within their communities. Find like-minded friends. Find un-like-minded friends. Explore every nook and cranny of your environment and discover where you belong and what you're inspired to do. Growing up, I often felt like an oddball but eventually found my way to a loving, inspiring community of artists, creatives, and, yes, geeks. You are never alone.

I want to thank Roaring Brook for giving me the dream opportunity to write a book about a subject that is both powerful and controversial. I hope this book motivates you to tell your story and to go out and make your mark. It's okay to be a little off the wall . . .

Richmond, VA

5 Pointz, New York City

Houston, TX

Paris